Were You Born a Dragon?

A story by Steve Dragon (really!)

Were You Born a Dragon?

Story by Steve Dragon
Illustrations by
Catherine McMahon

Rachel was a
very special girl.

When her Pop-Pop saw her for
the first time he said she was the
most beautiful baby he had ever
seen. And he should know
because he had four babies of his
own and Rachel was his fourth
grand baby.

Rachel Katherine was indeed a special baby.

Rachel Katherine Dragon was born a dragon.

You know, the kind that breathes fire. But she is not ready to yet. Her time will come when she could become one.

Rachel's mother and father were proud to have a new baby girl. But they were also worried about what would lie ahead of her.

Before she could be granted the powers of flight and fire she must first be taken to the Land of Dragons.

There Zargon, the King of Dragons, would give his approval for the new baby dragon to be given the powers.

Most people don't know it, but dragons live among everyone else on the planet.

They have jobs and own houses and cars like everyone else.

You just don't know who is a dragon and who isn't, do you?

People who are dragons can change into dragons once they turn 13 years old and during the light of a full moon

But before they get the power to
transform they must first meet
with Zargon when they are first
born.
If Zargon deems them worthy, he
will grant them the power to
become a real dragon.

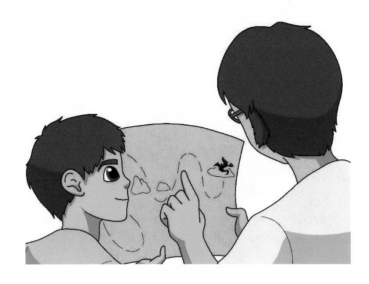

So one night Rachel's Dad and her big brother Steven made plans to take Rachel to the Land of Dragons.

It would be a long trip so Rachel's Mom packed them all a good lunch and a few extra bottles of formula and extra diapers for Rachel.

They bundled her up in heavy blankets to guard against the cold night air.

Steven was only seven and didn't
remember when his father took him
on his first trip to the Land of
Dragons.

Steven had seen his father transform
before so he wasn't scared by the
huge figure that now stood before
him.

He knew that this was an important time for Rachel, so he held her tight and after Dad became a dragon he climbed onto his father's back.

Some would be frightened by what some call a monster but Steven knew that his father would never hurt anyone. Unless they meant to harm any of his family.

So like Rachel's Pop-Pop Dragon did when her father was born the three dragons took off to fly to the Land of Dragons.

Not everyone knows where this is. Its secret has been kept from the public for many thousands of years. But those born as dragons know the way to go by following their instincts.

The trip would take several hours
but Steven knew he had to hold tight
to Rachel the whole way.

Along the way Dad thought of the day
he took Steven to see Zargon. His Dad,
Rachel and Steven's Pop-Pop, flew
alongside to help him when he arrived
at the island.

Since Dad had never been there as a grown-up Pop-Pop Dragon helped him once they landed. He told him where to go and what to do once they arrived at Zargon's palace.

Dad wished that his father could be with him this time but age was catching up with the elder Dragon. He couldn't make the hard and long trip this time.

Dad looked back and checked on
Steven and Rachel to make sure they
were safe and warm on his back. As
all children do, Steven asked several
times, "Are we there yet?"

Dad smiled a big dragon smile and a
puff of smoke came out of his nose
as he laughed at the question.
"Soon" was his answer every time.

He knew it was hard for Steven to keep a tight grip on both Rachel and his father as they flew over mountains and oceans to get to the Land of Dragons. And Steven knew how important it was to make sure she arrived safely.

Steven was amazed at how small
everything looked from his perch on
his father's back.
"Is that Hawaii?" he asked.

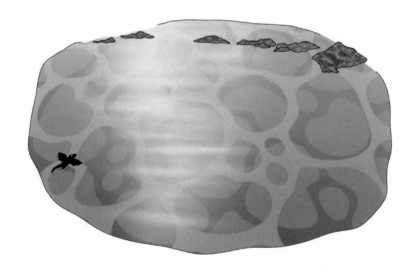

Indeed they were flying over Hawaii.

Steven was looking forward to his 13th birthday even though it was six years in the future. His Dad was teaching him what he needed to know when his time comes to become a real dragon.

Now he wants to help teach Rachel what she will need before her time arrives. He wanted to be a good big brother.

Along the way they stopped on an island to take a break, eat lunch and feed and change Rachel.

When they were done Dad changed back into a dragon and Steven once again held onto Rachel and his father as they took flight.

Soon afterwards they landed in the Land of Dragons where they were met by Arnod, the Chief Guard of Dragons.

"Who is this?" he roared. Steven
covered Rachel as best he could,
making sure that the fire and smoke
that came out with those words did
not get near his baby sister.

"This is Rachel, our newest dragon,"
answered her Dad.
"She is only two days old and we
requested a meeting with Zargon to get
his blessing to raise her as a dragon." He
showed a copy of the e-mail he sent two
days ago.

"Wait here" said Arnod, keeping a watchful eye on the three as he walked towards Zargon's throne room.

When he returned a few minutes later
he walked them into a large room with a
ceiling that, to Steven, looked as big as
the sky. "It has to be so that Zargon can
fly around in here" explained Dad.

Rachel started to cry as they reached the King's throne and Arnod told them to keep the child quiet. "She's hungry" explained Steven. "Leave her alone" he yelled.

Arnod turned toward Steven and Rachel, raised his head and looked like he was ready to breathe fire on them when Dad stepped in between them which stopped the guard in his tracks.

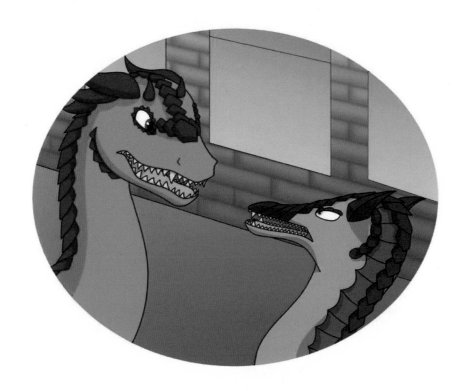

"She's just a baby" he said. "They do
that when they are hungry."
"She's a human baby and that's bad
enough" Arnod roared again.

Just then Zargon entered the room.
Arnod and Dad knelt in the presence
of the King and Dad told Steven to
do the same.

He tried hard to do so and hold his
sister close to him. He almost fell
over as he knelt down.

Dad and Zargon said hello to each other and the King asked why they had not seen each other since Steven was born.

"I have been busy with work and firefighting" Dad told the King. "And now that I have another child, I ask you grant the power of our ancestors and to allow her to transform when she is old enough."

"That's right," laughed Zargon. "We all have the power of fire and you spend your time putting out fires."

"I tell people who don't know my real self that I am making up for the sins of my ancestors," Dad said. "They laugh not knowing the whole truth.

Steven yelled to his Dad to warn him that Arnod was walking towards them again with a very mean look on his face.

Zargon told Arnod to leave the children alone and for the children not to worry; they were safe in his company.

"Let me see the baby dragon" he
said to Steven. Steven gently handed
Rachel to Zargon who held her up
for all the other dragons who came
into the room to see.

"I can see why her grandfather Dragon called her beautiful," he exclaimed. "She will be a great dragon one day and she has my blessing. I believe she will become a teacher."

Zargon then turned to Steven and told him, "It is your job to protect her and help teach her the ways of the dragons. It is your job to make sure she knows what it means to be a dragon and the history of your family."

"Do you promise to do so Steven?"

Steven answered, "Yes sir, I do."

Zargon gently handed Rachel back to
Steven and patted him on the head.
It was the first time he felt a
dragon's claw on his head but once
again he was not scared.

Dad thanked Zargon for his time and blessing and promised that they would all return to the Land of Dragons every year on Rachel's birthday.

Steven packed up what was left of their food and diapers and wrapped up Rachel tight and warm for the flight home. After all he did promise Zargon he would be a good big brother.

He thought about the day he would be able to carry Rachel on their yearly trip.

As they took off for home Arnod roared and breathed fire in their direction as his way of saying good riddance.

When they arrived home the next
day Steven ran to his mother. He
told her all about their trip including
the mean dragon who tried to hurt
his sister.

He told her how he stood up to Arnod and earned the respect of Zargon by protecting Rachel.

Mom smiled and shook her head.
Dad assured her that it really
happened that way. Mom gave
Steven a big hug and thanked him
for protecting the newest member
of their family.
She was glad he loved his little sister
as much as they did.

"But remember", Pop Pop Dragon
said. "You have to keep it all a
secret, for only dragons can know
about the Land of Dragons."

And what about you?

Were you born a dragon?

For Rachel, our special Dragon

Love,

Dad